The KIDS' Guide

ANTI-BULLYING

W
FRANKLIN WATTS
LONDON • SYDNEY

First published in Great Britain in 2022
by Hodder & Stoughton

Copyright © Hodder & Stoughton Limited, 2022

All rights reserved

Editor: Victoria Brooker
Design: Thy Bui
Illustrator: Scott Garrett

ISBN: 978 1 4451 8136 3 (hbk)
ISBN: 978 1 4451 8137 0 (pbk)

Printed in China

Franklin Watts
An imprint of Hachette Children's Group
Part of Hodder & Stoughton
Carmelite House
50 Victoria Embankment
London EC4Y 0DZ

An Hachette UK Company
www.hachette.co.uk
www.hachettechildrens.co.uk

INTRODUCTION

You may be reading this book because you are being bullied. Or maybe you know a person who is being bullied and you want to help them. Perhaps you're worried that you're bullying someone and you want to stop ...

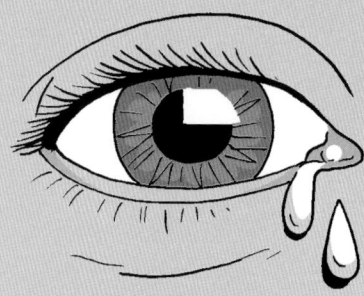

Bullying is when actions or words are used to hurt someone or make them feel bad. Bullying is when a person or people hurt someone on purpose and repeat their cruelty again and again.

When you're being bullied it can feel like nothing can help and nobody understands. It can make you feel miserable and helpless. It can feel like the bullying will

n
e
v
e
r
e
n
d ...

Being bullied can feel like you're in a dark place with no one there beside you and no hope of escape. But there is light at the end of the tunnel! You just have to keep moving towards it ...

EFFECTS OF BULLYING

Bullying affects everyone in different ways. People may feel ...

**angry and cross,
violent and frustrated,**

**scared and fearful,
threatened and unsafe,**

**weak, powerless
and worthless,
embarrassed
or ashamed,**

**sad and
unhappy,
lonely and lost.**

BE A FEELINGS DETECTIVE

Bullying can affect anyone, anywhere.

Be a feelings detective and follow the clues to see if there are warning signs that you're being bullied.

If you said YES to any of these things, you may be being bullied. Trust your feelings. If someone makes you feel bad, they are doing something wrong! Speak to an adult about what is happening.

FRIEND OR FOE?

Bullying happens in different ways. Sometimes bullying is hard to spot because it's someone you think is a friend.

You can't tell if someone might bully you just by looking at them. It's what they do that counts. Are they friend or frenemy?

Friends encourage you and make you feel good.

Friends make you laugh.

Friends care about what you say and how you feel.

Friends stick up for you.

A frenemy is someone you think is a friend but who actually isn't kind to you. When friends upset you, they say sorry and don't do it again.

PHYSICAL BULLYING

Physical bullying is easier to spot than some forms of bullying. Physical bullying includes things such as kicking, pinching, hair pulling or the threat of violence. Threats of violence may not physically hurt you but they can make you feel very scared and under attack.

> Every day they shove me or kick me when they go past, or snatch my books.

> I get told I'll be beaten up if I don't hand over my lunch money.

> I hate going to school and I feel shaky and sick as soon as I wake up in the mornings.

Being physically hurt or injured by someone can make people feel very, very

ANGRY.

It can make people feel as if they want to hit back. Don't. You could get badly hurt or blamed for starting the trouble. Keep yourself safe and try to remove yourself from the situation and find help in an adult you trust.

The problem is if I hit back it could get worse …

NAME CALLING AND TEASING

Teasing and name calling may not hurt people physically, but they hurt feelings badly. Some people may say they're only joking or having a laugh when they tease or taunt others. But if teasing or name calling persists and hurts your feelings, it is bullying. And bullying is no joke.

He says rude things about me whenever he gets a chance.

She shouts a nasty nickname across the playground.

He always makes me the butt of his so-called jokes.

She taunts me about the clothes I wear.

It can be very hard to ignore the nasty things someone says. It can get inside your head and start to make you feel like there really is something wrong with you. There isn't. Give yourself the advice you'd give a bullied friend: You're great and they are just trying to hurt you – don't let them!

Sometimes I try to pretend I have an invisible forcefield around me that the insults bounce off.

LEFT OUT AND FEELING ALONE

It's not nice to feel left out of games, groups and conversation or like you're being prevented from making friends.

> He invited everyone else in our class to a party except me.

> She gets other people to pretend they don't hear me when I speak.

> He tells people I said bad things about them so they stop talking to me.

> She always makes sure I'm left out of games.

This kind of bullying is often silent and secretive. They might whisper lies or mean things about someone.

This kind of bullying can make a person feel like everyone else is talking about them or laughing at them. It can make them feel left out and alone, as if they're trapped on a desert island and no one wants to rescue them.

CYBERBULLYING

Lots of bullying today happens online – on social media, in text groups, or via mobile phones. This is known as cyberbullying.

> Everyone HATES you.

> You're such a LOSER.

> You need BEATING UP.

Threatening text messages or other forms of cyberbullying can drop at any time of the day or night on any day of the week. Cyberbullying follows victims wherever they go. It can feel like there's no escape from the bullying.

The other horrible thing about cyberbullying is that it can be done anonymously. A person can use fake IDs and screen names or hide their number so you don't know who they are.

The victim is left wondering who is responsible for it. This can make it hard to trust anyone and start to suspect everyone of being the one who sent that hateful message ...

BUT electronic messages CAN be traced. Make sure to print and keep records of all cyberbullying incidents so they can be tracked down – even if they think they are hiding.

ADULTS WHO BULLY

Most adults who look after and teach or train young people are kind, caring and respectful. They do all they can to prevent bullying. Sadly, there are a few adults who do bully.

I'm not good at maths and my teacher is always trying to humiliate me in front of the class.

My coach says I'm fat and calls me nasty nicknames to make the rest of my team laugh.

Parents, teachers and trainers may get cross and hand out punishments sometimes, but that's okay if their criticism is justified. However, if an adult uses their position of power to insult, punish or embarrass you in an unreasonable way, that is bullying. If an adult is bullying you, that's a very serious issue, which you need to get sorted as soon as you can.

My dad always takes his anger out on me. He hits me if I don't do as I'm told fast enough.

PREJUDICE AND RACISM

People who bully mostly pick on people for no reason at all. Some repeatedly attack someone because that person is different to them in a particular way. This is called

PREJUDICE.

Someone might pick on people who live a different way of life to them. Another might attack someone because of their religion or because they love others of the same sex as them.

Some people pick on others because of the colour of their skin, their family background or because their family comes from a different country. This is called racism.

Bullying someone because of their gender, sexuality, religious beliefs, race, skin colour or because they have a disability, is hate crime and is against the law.

If this is happening to you or a young person you know, you or they can report it online (see pages 46–47 for details). If you feel in danger, you can also contact the police.

GOOD ADVICE

Kids who were bullied in the past have lots of advice for kids being bullied today ...

Q How can I get help?

A Tell an adult about the bullying as soon as you can. It is hard to stop bullying without help.

Q How can I stay safe walking home?

A I used to ask friends to walk with me so I was never alone.

Q What should I say when someone insults me?

A I used to pretend I didn't hear and walked away, leaving them standing there.

Q How can I hurt a bully back when he's pushing me around?

A Never fight back. You'll make things worse. Walk away and find help from an adult. If you can't get away, then shout STOP really loudly!

It's a great idea to ignore and avoid bullying if you can, but always ask for help. Write down every incident that happens, however small. You can use this as evidence when you report the bullying.

TACKLING CYBERBULLYING

Cyberbullying is a problem and everyone needs to know how to take action against it.

- ♥ Set up privacy settings and allow only people you trust to see your pages.
- ♥ Post a picture of an animal instead of yourself.

- ➡ Set up private chatrooms for you and your friends.
- ➡ Avoid using your real name in other chatrooms or gaming groups.
- ➡ Never give personal details like addresses or phone numbers.
- ➡ If bullying happens, leave the group.

Keep ALL of your passwords top secret.

Give your number only to people you trust.

Never reply to people you don't know and trust.

Block them or change your number so they can't contact you again.

Report bullying to your mobile phone company.

TALK, TALK, TALK ...

These suggestions can all help and you might want to try some of them, but THE most important thing that anyone who has ever been bullied will tell you to do is to ...

... TALK

Not telling only helps the bully. Bullying thrives on secrecy. Telling people and getting help from others is the very best way to take away their power.

ABOUT IT!

STEPS IN THE RIGHT DIRECTION

It can be hard to take the first step. So here are some tips for talking and telling about bullying …

1 Decide who is the best adult to help you: a parent or guardian, teacher or friend, or a professional, such as a counsellor?

2 Write down what has happened. Gather any evidence you have, such as photos of bruises, screenshots of hate messages etc …

3 Find a time when you can have your chosen adult's undivided attention. It doesn't have to be face-to-face – you can call, message or video chat too.

Let the person know if you want advice, practical support or just someone to listen.

5

4

When talking about a tough topic, focus on using 'I' statements and be specific. For example, 'I feel upset when ...'

6

Don't give up. If the first adult you speak to doesn't help, find someone else to give you the support you need.

This is all great advice if you're planning to talk to someone but it's also fine to just jump in at the deep end and blurt it all out to anyone who'll listen! The important thing is to **TALK ABOUT IT** in any way and to anyone that suits you.

ELI's STORY

Eli had been bullied for a long time. They knew they had to do something about it, but they were embarrassed and also scared by the threats of the person bullying.

Stop whining and keep quiet – no one will believe you anyway ...

You don't want people to think you're a snitch, do you?

Eli didn't tell Dad because they were scared Dad would storm into school and make a big scene. Eli felt SO helpless ... They didn't know how much more of the bullying they could stand ...

Eli was getting so worried about going to school they lost their appetite. Dad noticed and sat beside Eli.

Eli felt tears falling down their cheeks. Eli started sobbing uncontrollably. It was like all those weeks of hurt from the bullying that had been held tight inside just flooded out in one go.

Dad listened quietly and calmly while Eli told him everything that happened. He hugged Eli for a long time. Then they sat together and made a plan to stop the bullying.

SCHOOL HELP

They got an appointment with Eli's teacher after school. Eli showed phone messages they'd been sent. The teacher was very kind and understanding. She said it took courage to report the bullying.

After an investigation, the person bullying Eli was told off and it was explained to them that their behaviour was unacceptable. Eli and the person who had done the bullying were brought together so the person bullying could say sorry and they could agree a way forward together.

Eli still feels a bit anxious about school some days. But on a good day Eli also feels …

BRAVE,

PROUD,

CONFIDENT,

POWERFUL.

The really important thing is that Eli no longer feels alone. They know if there is a problem they can talk to Dad or the teacher at any time and they can get HELP.

WHY DO PEOPLE BULLY?

People bully for reasons that usually have nothing to do with the people they pick on!

Many people bully others because they have been bullied or hurt themselves. Some people bully others to get attention because they don't get enough attention at home. Some bully others to make themselves feel more popular.

Sometimes people use violence to make themselves feel bigger and more powerful. Some people bully to vent their anger or unhappiness about problems in their own lives.

Bullying can be part of a chain reaction and an endless cycle of problems ...

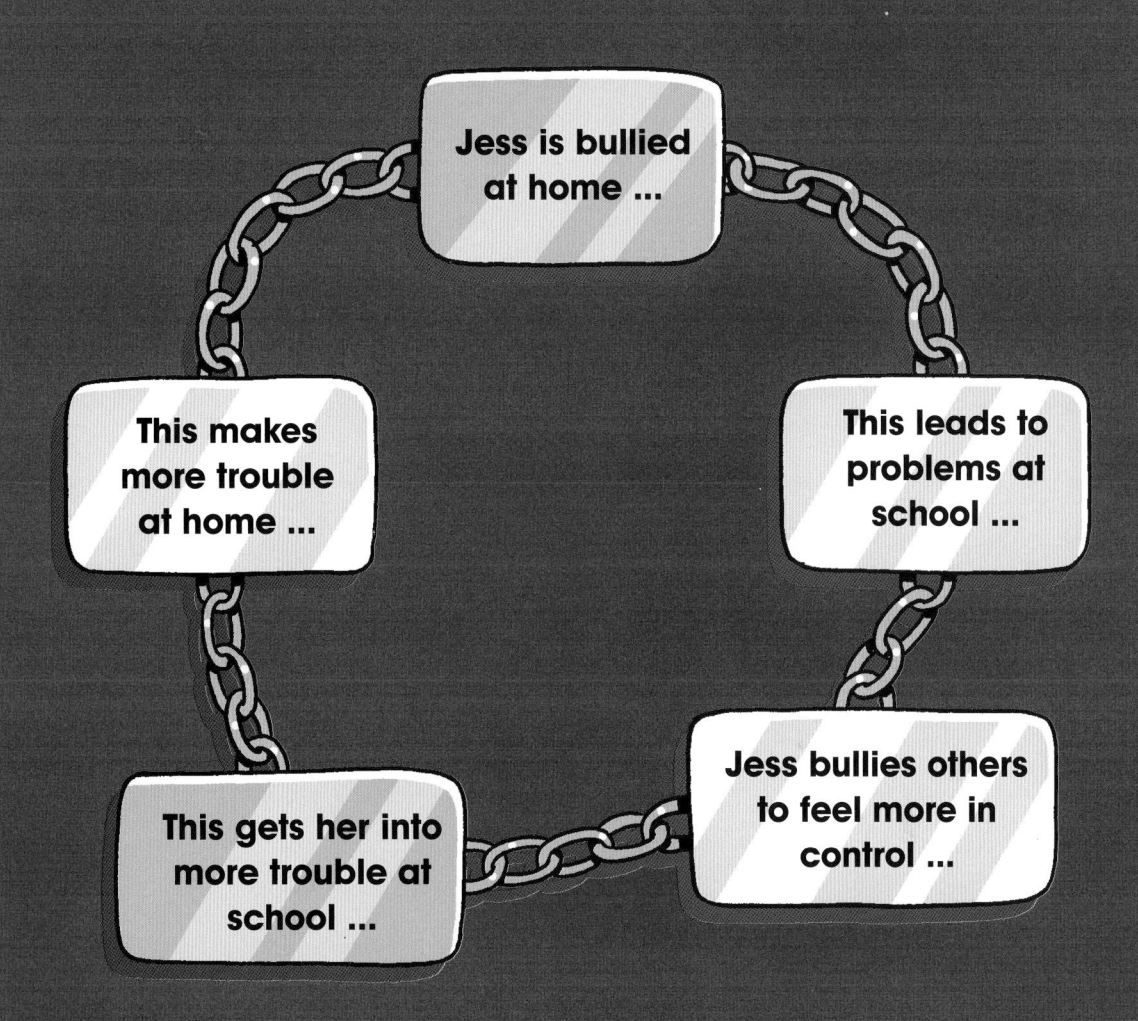

- Jess is bullied at home ...
- This leads to problems at school ...
- Jess bullies others to feel more in control ...
- This gets her into more trouble at school ...
- This makes more trouble at home ...

Recognising that people who bully have problems of their own can make them seem less powerful.

TIME TO STOP BULLYING

No one is born a bully. Bullying is a behaviour people learn, and it can be unlearned as easily as it was learned.

Try the following actions to solve the puzzle of why you bully and stop it.

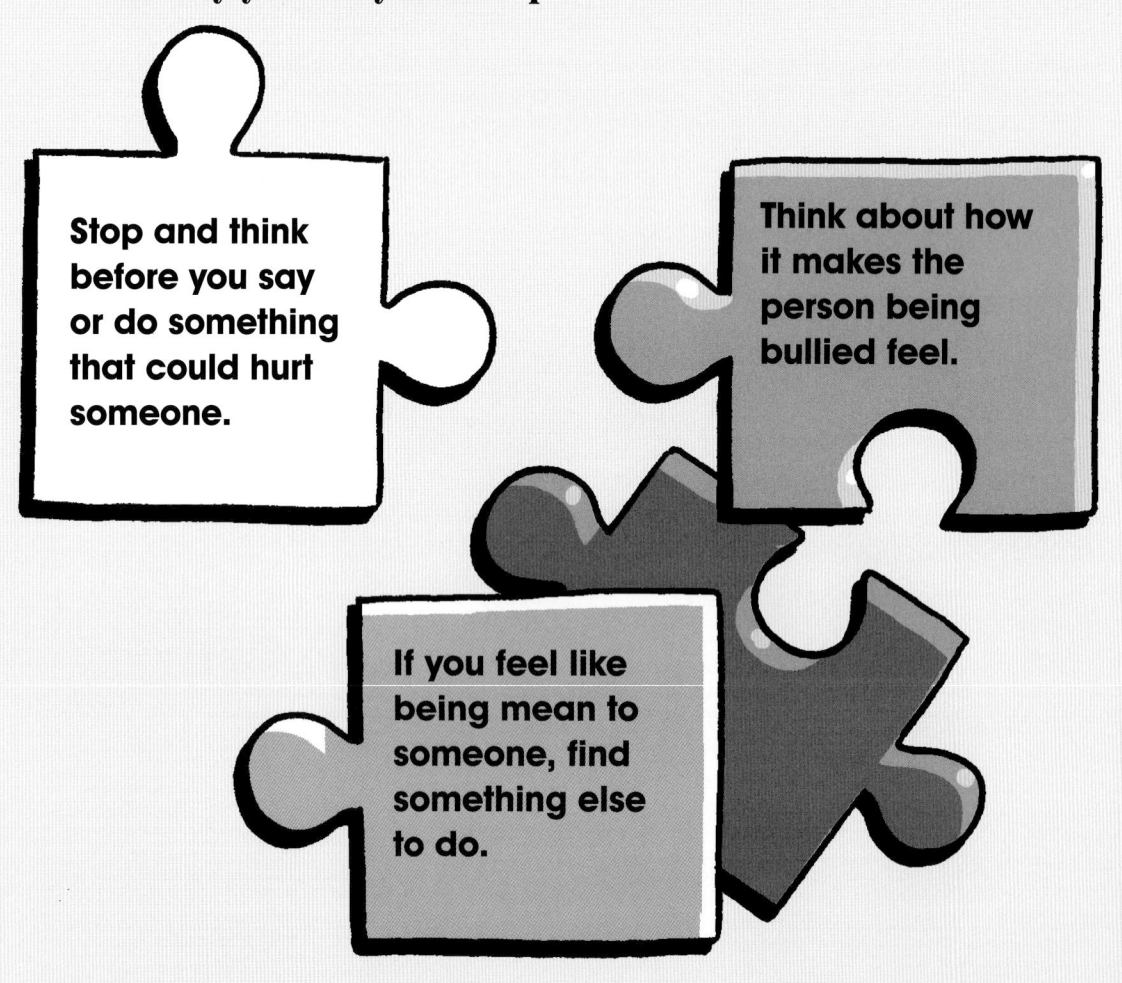

Stop and think before you say or do something that could hurt someone.

Think about how it makes the person being bullied feel.

If you feel like being mean to someone, find something else to do.

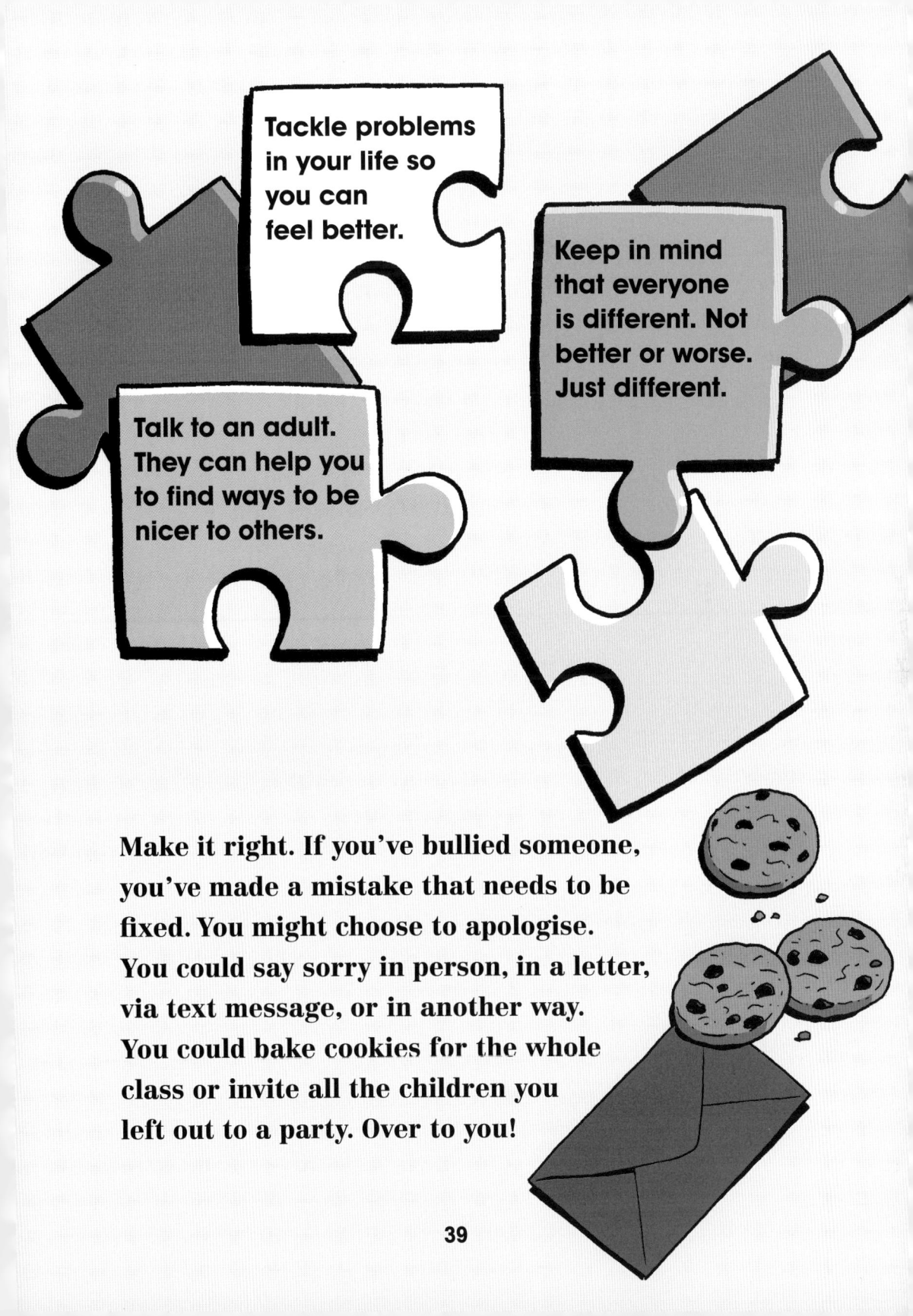

Tackle problems in your life so you can feel better.

Keep in mind that everyone is different. Not better or worse. Just different.

Talk to an adult. They can help you to find ways to be nicer to others.

Make it right. If you've bullied someone, you've made a mistake that needs to be fixed. You might choose to apologise. You could say sorry in person, in a letter, via text message, or in another way. You could bake cookies for the whole class or invite all the children you left out to a party. Over to you!

HEALING AFTER BULLYING

Even when the bullying stops, the hurt might not stop for someone who has been bullied. Bullying can damage your self-esteem – your good feelings about yourself. But there are things you can do to build yourself back up again ...

BE NICE TO YOU. Do something you love every day. If it makes you happy, make time for it.

BE POSITIVE. Block out negative thoughts. Focus on what's good about you and your life. Write down three of these things each day.

GO FOR IT! You can get a real buzz and sense of achievement from taking on a new hobby or challenge.

MOVE IT!
Exercise, especially outdoors, is a great way to build confidence. Breaking a sweat also releases feel-good chemicals called endorphins, which make you feel happier.

CALL A FRIEND. Find people who make you feel good about yourself and avoid those who don't.

DON'T COMPARE! Focus on your own goals and achievements, rather than measuring them against someone else's.

STAND TOGETHER

We can all say NO to bullying!

Here are some ideas for things we can all do to stop bullying in its tracks.

Don't become an audience for bullying. Turn or walk away when they bully someone.

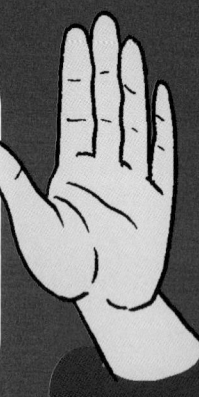

Shift the focus from the victim and redirect attention elsewhere.

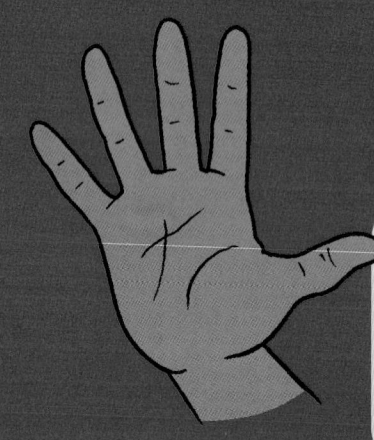

Never laugh or smile at mean jokes – it just encourages them.

Talk to the victim so they don't feel alone and maybe ask them to join a game.

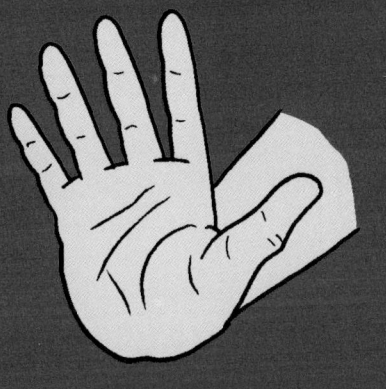

Tell an adult. Get help!

If you feel safe doing so, tell the person bullying to stop.

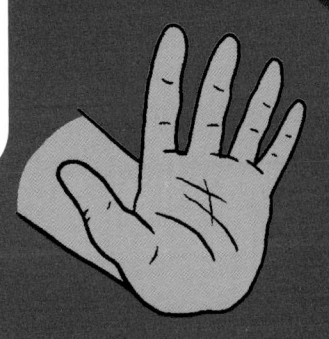

If we all **STAND TOGETHER AGAINST BULLYING,** we can make it stop.

BEYOND THE BULLYING

Bullying is bad for everyone. The person who is bullied, the people who see it happen and even the person bullying. This damage can take a long time to heal, but it does get better. One day soon you'll feel as if you're stepping out of that dark tunnel and into the bright, smiling sunlight again ...

Bullying is difficult to deal with and when you ask for help, it still may not stop immediately. The most important thing is never to give up. Keep ignoring and avoiding, keep talking and telling. Keep taking care of yourself, focusing on who and what makes you feel good and building your self-esteem.

Never lose heart. Most people who have been bullied agree that talking was the thing that helped them more than anything else. It can take time but, with help, things will get better.

You will feel safe again.
You will feel happy again.

Some people even say that bullying made them a braver, wiser and more confident person.

FURTHER INFORMATION

HELPLINES

If it feels awkward talking to somebody you know, there are organisations with helplines who will point you in the right direction.

ChildLine provides a confidential free 24-hour helpline for children in trouble or danger. Call 0800 1111 or ask questions online at: www.childline.org.uk

YouthtoYouth's helpline is run by young people for young people aged 11-19. Call the YouthtoYouth helpline on 020 8896 3675. Visit their website at: www.youthtoyouth.co.uk to find out more.

This Youth Access website provides names of local youth counsellors: www.youthaccess.org.uk

COUNSELLORS
Sometimes it's easier to talk with a stranger about your problems. Talking one-to-one in private allows you to open up in a safe environment.

USEFUL WEBSITES

ANTI-BULLYING ALLIANCE's website has lots of advice about bullying and where you can go to get help.
https://anti-bullyingalliance.org.uk/tools-information/advice-and-support/if-youre-being-bullied

CHILDLINE's website has answers to questions such as 'I am a bully, what can I do?' and 'My teacher is bullying me, what can I do?'
www.childline.org.uk/explore/bullying/pages/bullying.aspx

KIDSCAPE's website has useful information for young people, parents, carers and professionals.
www.kidscape.org.uk

INDEX

adults 20–21, 30, 31, 39, 43
anger 6, 13, 20, 21, 36
appetite (loss) 9, 33

bruises 9, 30

chatrooms 18, 26
confidence 9, 41
counsellors 30, 46
cyberbullying 18–19, 26–27

emotions 6, 7
evidence (of bullying) 19, 25, 30
exercise 41

feelings 5, 6, 7, 8, 9, 14, 16, 40
fighting 13, 25
frenemies 10–11
friends 10, 11, 15, 16, 26, 30, 41

games 16, 43
gender 23

hate crime 23
hitting 13, 21
hurt (feeling and being) 4, 12, 13, 14, 15, 25, 33, 36, 38, 40

insults 15, 21, 25

joking 14, 42

loneliness 5, 6, 17

nicknames 14, 20

online bullying 18–19, 26-27

parents 21, 30, 34, 36

racism 22–23
religion 22, 23

school 9, 12, 32, 33, 34–35, 37
secrets 10, 11, 17, 28
self-esteem 7, 40, 44
sexuality 22, 23
skin colour 22, 23
social media 18
sorry (saying) 11, 39

teachers 20, 21, 24, 30, 34, 35

victims (of bullying) 18, 19, 42, 43
violence 12–13, 36